For Cale and Bryndon, my favorite storytellers. – M.F.

To my family for being patient and understanding. – O.V.

STERLING CHILDREN'S BOOKS
New York

An Imprint of Sterling Publishing
1166 Avenue of the Americas
New York, NY 10036

~~My Story of Me~~

~~The Legend of Salty Pete~~

~~The Chronicle of Intergalactic Conquest~~

~~A Tale of Foul Dragons and Fair Maidens~~

WHOSE STORY IS THIS, ANYWAY?

by Mike Flaherty · illustrated by Oriol Vidal

STERLING CHILDREN'S BOOKS
New York

You want to hear a story? I've got a great one.

Why is it great?
Because it's all about me.

This is my cat, Emperor Falafel.

My favorite place is the beach, where I can build a sand palace for Emperor Falafel, even though he doesn't really like the sand, and—

Hey, what's going on here?
Arr, if ye don't mind, ye be interruptin' The Legend of Salty Pete.

The Legend of Salty Pete?
Salty Pete, that be me, and this be me legend. Though, I might call it Hijinks on the High Seas.
I can't decide.

ROOOOOWAR!
Whoa, whoa, whoa. Hold on.
My story doesn't have dinosaurs.

It's not a legend. It's just a story about me. There aren't any pirates or dinosaurs in it.
Hmm. Your story could definitely use more dinosaurs. And maybe you could put a hot dog stand in this story.
I'm *starving*.

HO, PEASANTS!
You have got to be kidding me . . .
I am Sir Knightly! Gather, and heed my epic tale of gallant knights, foul dragons, and fair maidens!

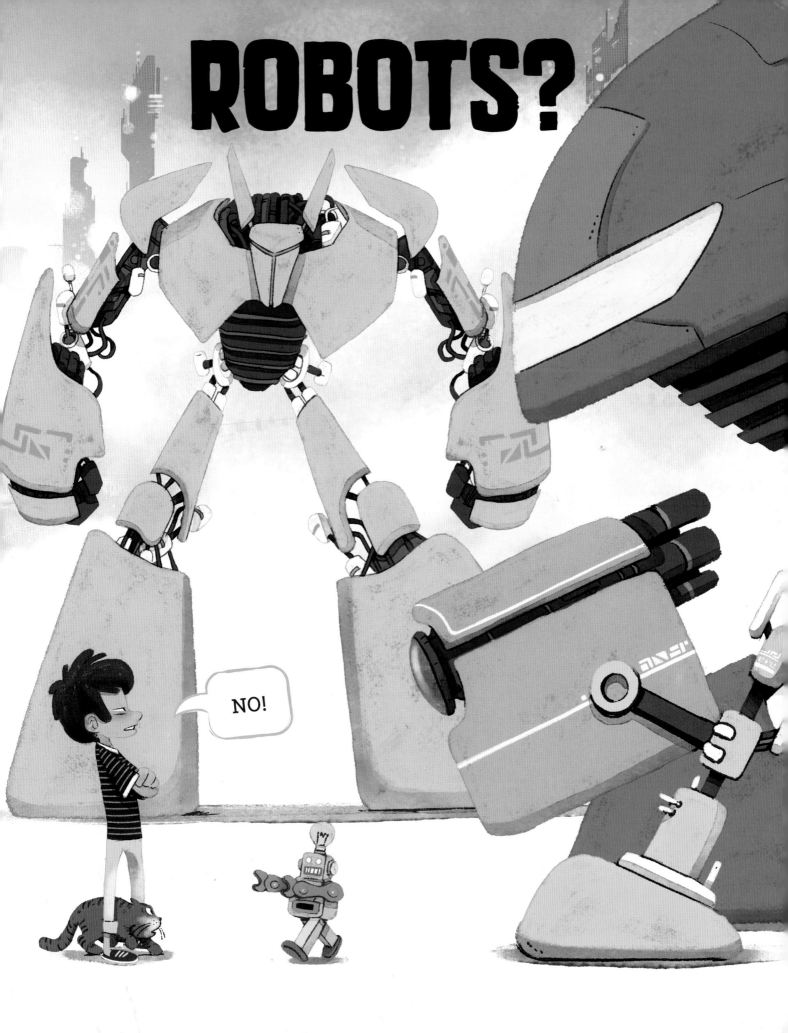

Whew, finally. Now we can get back to my story.
Where were we? Oh, yeah, the beach. So . . .

Wait a second, did you just yawn?
This isn't a bedtime story.
Are you . . . bored?

Don't you want to hear about me?
Emperor Falafel? Isn't that exciting?

Let me guess.
You'd rather hear a story
with pirates and knights or
aliens and dinosaurs.
I guess those guys did have
some pretty cool stories, too.
Alright, fine . . .

So, this is my story about me . . .

. . . and the day I met a bunch of crazy new friends.